For Mam, Dad & Kerry. . .

T.C xx

WILLOW VALLEY

STUMPY'S STYLE

BUTTON-OAK MILL

POPPY FIELD

PODRICK HARE'S HOUSE

TEN OAKS FIELD

ALLOTMENTS

BUTTERCUP MEADOW

MOSSY HOLLOW

HORATIO'S HOUSE

WILLOUGHBY WHITE-WHISKERS' HOUSE

ACORNS SCHOOL

LIBRARY

BLUEBELL WOOD

VILLAGE SQUARE

BAKERS

STARLA'S HOUSE

TOY SHOP

HOOT HILL BARN

MUMFORD MOLE'S HOUSE

THE DARK WOOD

MARTHA RABBIT'S HOUSE

OLD CROOKED STONE BRIDGE

RILEY'S HOUSE

Chapter 1

It was a bright, sunny morning in Willow Valley. Butterflies danced through meadows of clover, birds sang in the trees, and shimmering dragonflies fluttered over the river.

The cave-houses dotted on the rolling green hills all had their doors open wide as happy little animals pattered out to play in the sunshine.

Some were clutching skipping ropes. Others rolled large wooden hoops.

"Let's make daisy chains!" shouted a floppy-eared bunny.

But not everyone was hurrying out to play. Riley, a little toffee-coloured mouse, was going on holiday today. *And* he was taking his two best friends – Starla, a smiley, fluffy-faced badger and a roly-poly hedgehog called Horatio Spark.

They were down at Willow Valley railway station, waiting for their train. Riley's grandfather, Percy Lightfoot, was going with them too. For *weeks* he and Riley had been planning this holiday together.

They were going to stay with Riley's Aunt Marigold and Uncle Norton in Cockleshell Bay, which was by the sea. Riley had stayed with his aunt and uncle before, but it was Starla and Horatio's first time. Riley couldn't wait to show them the caves and fish for crabs in the rock pools! It was going to be the best summer holiday *ever*.

"What time is it, Grandpa?" Riley asked.

"Almost ten o'clock," Grandpa smiled.

"Oooh!" squealed Horatio, bobbing up and down. "Our train will be here any minute now."

"Hooray!" cheered Starla. She felt like she could burst with excitement!

Riley's mum and his little sister, Mimi-Rose, had come to wave them off. Mimi-Rose was wearing a sparkly tiara and clutching a starry wand. She didn't look terribly happy, though. "It's not fair that I'm too little to go!" she frowned.

On the dot of ten o'clock, a big green steam train came rolling into the station, puffing out clouds of fluffy white smoke into the clear blue sky. "Look!" cried Horatio, pointing a paw. "It's here!"

Horatio loved summer holidays *nearly* as much as he loved ginger cake. In fact, Horatio loved *many* things, most of which got him into trouble! He never meant any harm, though. He just liked to *do* things, that was all. . .

Riley said goodbye to his mum and little sister. Mimi-Rose hugged and hugged him and it felt like she'd never let go.

Finally, Riley wriggled from her grip. "But I want to go too," his little sister sniffed.

"Maybe next year," said their mum.

Starla promised she'd bring Mimi-Rose back some shells that she could use to make pretty necklaces.

"But I *still* can't splash in the sea. . ." Mimi-Rose sighed.

Starla thought for a moment. "Or while we're away you could help my grandpa on the *Kingfisher*!"

Mimi-Rose's ears pricked up at once. She liked helping out – it made her feel important – and she *especially* liked helping out on the boats!

There were three narrowboats in Willow Valley. One was the *Kingfisher*, and the other two were called the *Whirligig* and the *Dragonfly*. The animals used these boats to sail downriver on their market trips to sell their lovely home-made goods. Everybody loved these trips because they were so much fun!

Starla's grandpa, Willoughby White-Whiskers, was the captain of the fleet, so he was in charge of all the boats. They had just come back from their summer trip, so now the boats would need to be cleaned and tidied.

"OK!" nodded Mimi-Rose, brightening up. "I'll be the captain's helper! Last time I helped Mr White-Whiskers, he gave me hot chocolate!"

Suddenly the guard blew his whistle, so Riley and his friends hurried on to the train. Grandpa found their seats and as the train moved off they waved goodbye through the window.

"*Yippee!*" cheered Riley, Starla and Horatio. They were on their way to the seaside at last!

As the train chugged out of Willow Valley, Riley glimpsed Buttonoak Mill, then the three narrowboats on the river.

Willoughby White-Whiskers waved from the *Kingfisher* as their train tootled past. "It's Grandpa, look!" cried Starla, waving back wildly.

They saw meadows dotted with buttercups and poppies, and bumpy green hills filled with trees. Set into the hills were little stony cave-houses. The Willow Valley animals lived in these. Riley could see Martha Rabbit outside hers, hanging up her washing to dry.

They passed gardens brimming with foxgloves and hollyhocks, and fruit trees full of apples and plums.

Horatio pointed out Podrick Hare
pulling up his prize-winning cabbages.

"Bye bye, Willow Valley!" giggled the
three best friends as their train trundled
away.

As they travelled on, the hills became softer and the fields looked square and neat. The train was going faster now through the open countryside. They whizzed past meadows of mooing cows and sheep as fluffy as rainclouds!

"Hey, let's play a game," Horatio cried. He said that the train's billowing smoke reminded him of a dragon. "We can pretend we're flying on a dragon called Dylan!"

The game began and it was great fun. They pretended they were knights flying off on their dragon to battle a grumpy old sea monster. Horatio kept prodding

Riley with his spade, which he said was now his knight's sword.

"Take that! And that! *And that!*" he chuckled.

"Hey," giggled Riley, "*I'm* not the grumpy old monster!"

Riley now took out a board game. It was called Hopping Frogs. He and Mimi-Rose played it a lot at home.

The friends took it in turns to roll the dice and find the quickest way to the lily pad. Riley's frog, Hoppity, got back first. "Good job, Hoppity!" said Riley.

Horatio's frog, Boris, kept landing in the swamp, along with Starla's frog, called Freya. *"Plop!"* giggled Starla, as Freya landed in the mud yet again.

Before they knew it, it was time for lunch, so they shared out the goodies they'd brought.

Grandpa Lightfoot had cheese and chutney rolls. Riley had some pasties and pickles. Starla passed round some yummy tarts filled with raspberries and cream. Even Horatio managed to share out his "best *ever* ginger cake!"

They tied napkins around their necks and eagerly tucked in. As they ate, they talked about the things they wanted to do at the seaside.

"I'd like to stroll on the beach," said Grandpa, "and collect some nice bits of driftwood."

"I want to go to the *caves*!" cried Riley. He'd always wanted to be an explorer like his dad, Barty Black-Paw, had been. In the caves he'd be able to pretend he really *was* one – a brave explorer discovering a dark new land.

"Well, *I'm* going to catch a sea monster," said Horatio. "And dig for treasure, and leap over waves, and build a sandcastle – with a moat!" He looked at Starla. "What do you want to do?"

"I'd like to meet a mermaid," giggled

Starla. "She could teach me how to dive!" She told them she'd brought her mermaid book to read as well.

"Hey, Daisy might like my book!" said Starla.

"I bet she won't," Riley whispered. "Daisy's probably really frightened of mermaids."

Daisy was Riley's cousin and a real worry-wart. Her family all loved her very much, but sometimes they wished she'd be a bit more adventurous.

Starla and Horatio had met Daisy when she'd come to Willow Valley on holiday.

"Oh, I remember her *now*," groaned Horatio quietly, so Riley's grandpa didn't hear. Percy Lightfoot was Daisy's grandfather too because Riley's mum and Daisy's mum were sisters.

Riley thought back to last summer when Daisy had been staying with him. She hadn't wanted to play in the garden in case she got stung by nettles. She'd trembled when they'd picnicked near the river, in case she toppled in and drowned. And when Horatio had suggested *tightrope walking*, Daisy had fled to her room and hidden under the bed!

"She was just a bit timid," said Starla kindly. "She might be braver now."

"Hmmm," said Riley with a shrug. He hoped so. . .

With that, the train gave a cheery toot as it neared Cockleshell Bay. "Hey, we're almost there!" cried Riley.

"Hooray!" cheered Starla.

They peered through the window as the train chugged along the pretty, winding coast. Riley pointed to the clear blue sea. "Look – the waves are *huge*!" he cried.

Suddenly the train whooshed into a tunnel and it went as black as night.

"Woohoo!" cried Horatio. This was *so* exciting!

When they came out the other side the sea had disappeared. Now all they could see were rows of houses, and shops selling ice cream and kites.

"Look!" squeaked Riley. "We're coming into the station!"

With that the train began to slow down and everyone gathered up their things. Finally it came to a stop with a long, low *hissssssssss*.

Grandpa Lightfoot led them off the train on to a neat platform. It had a white picket fence, flowers in pots and it smelled of sunshine and the sea.

Aunt Marigold, Uncle Norton and Daisy were waiting on the platform to meet them. Daisy was holding a fluffy seal teddy very tightly.

"So good to see you!" Aunt Marigold beamed, her deep golden fur glistening.

"Hello!" said Uncle Norton with a cheery wave.

"Hi there," cried everyone, and then Grandpa Lightfoot gave little Daisy a hug. "Good to see you, Daisy!" he smiled.

"Hello, Grandpa," squeaked Daisy.

Daisy was dainty and, like Mimi-Rose, was snowy white all over, except for a golden heart-shaped splodge on one ear.

Riley thought his cousin already looked worried. "Do you think it might thunder?" Daisy asked. She had spotted a *teeny* grey cloud in the sky.

"Nah," said Horatio. "It's boiling today!"

"Come on, then!" smiled Grandpa, taking Daisy's hand. "Off we go to Seashell Cottage!"

Chapter 2

Riley had a spring in his step as they headed out of the station and down the cobbled streets. The sun shone brightly and the sky was the colour of the cornflowers back home in Willow Valley. They really couldn't have wished for a lovelier day!

They walked on up a hilly street where the houses were tall and wonky. "How come they're so high?" Horatio asked.

"Well, everyone wants to see the sea," explained Aunt Marigold, "which is on the other side of the hill. So they build their houses as tall as giraffes to see it!"

"I wish *my* house was as tall as a giraffe," said Horatio.

"Oh, I don't!" Daisy gasped. "It might topple over in a storm! I like my house just the way it is. It's on the beach so *we* can see the sea any time. . ."

"Wow! You live on the *beach*?" cried Starla. "That must be so much fun! Daisy, have you ever spotted a mermaid?"

"Or a pirate?" Riley asked.

"Yeah!" cried Horatio. "There must be *tons* of pirates round here!"

Daisy quickly shook her head. "Oooh no!" she said. "I don't go on the beach much. I don't like to get too sandy or too wet. I prefer to stay home and play with all my seal teddies."

Five minutes later they arrived at the beach. It was just how Riley remembered it. Seagulls soared in the deep blue sky and the warm breeze tasted of salt.

"And look!" cried Riley. "There's Aunt Marigold's cottage!"

Seashell Cottage was made from hundreds of shells which twinkled in the afternoon sun. There were cockle shells and clam shells. There were conches and winkles.

The windows were lined with razor shells in shimmering shades of purple, and pretty scallop shells made up the roof, sitting in neat little rows, like opened-out fans.

"I wish *I* lived in a house like this!" said Starla. She whisked out her camera and took a quick photo to show her family back home.

The cottage stood on the golden sand,

which trickled through their toes. Sailing boats bobbed about on the sea as a gentle breeze puffed out their snow-white sails. The water was clear and the brightest blue Riley had ever seen, and playful waves scampered up and down the sand.

Riley and his friends couldn't wait to dip their toes in the water, but first they had to take their luggage inside.

Leading to the cottage were flower beds planted with catmint, pheasant grass and sea holly. "That holly looks as prickly as Horatio!" Grandpa Lightfoot laughed.

Riley's uncle opened the front door and everyone followed him in. The little cottage was *just* as lovely on the inside too. The walls were made of pearly white shells and the chairs had been carved out of driftwood. Yellow gingham curtains hung at the windows, a soft rug was spread on the floor, and pale purple catmint sat in a jug on the table.

"I love it here!" Starla cried.

"Just wait till you see upstairs," grinned Riley. "There are beds made out of rowing boats!"

"*Wow*," gasped Horatio.

While Aunt Marigold made afternoon tea, Daisy showed them upstairs. Riley and Horatio were sharing a bedroom, as were Starla and Daisy.

The boys' bedroom had curtains with crabs on and their wardrobe was in the shape of a lighthouse. Their bunk beds were real boats that you had to climb into, and the rug on the floor looked like a giant octopus.

"Whoa!" cried Horatio. "This is amazing!"

"I bagsy the top bunk!" giggled Riley. As they both made a dive for it, Daisy took Starla to their room.

"Oh," smiled Starla when they went inside. "It's so pretty!"

The girls' room had beds shaped like scallop shells and pretty orange starfish on the curtains. The bookcase was filled with books about seals and on Daisy's bed sat a row of little seal teddies.

"This is Twinkle!" Daisy said, scooping up a fluffy white one. Daisy lowered her voice. "She's my favourite."

Grandpa Lightfoot had the attic room to himself. He liked the model sailing boat which sat on the bedside table and the old brown sea maps in thick wooden frames on the walls.

Everyone unpacked their things, then went downstairs for tea. The table had been laid with a lacy cloth and on it was a pretty tea set. Aunt Marigold had gone to a lot of trouble to make them feel welcome.

Beside the jug of catmint there was

now a dainty teapot. But Horatio's eyes
were drawn to a cake stand loaded with
wonderful goodies. There were shell-
shaped pastries filled with cream. There
were biscuits that looked like seahorses.
Even the fairy cakes had sugar-paste
crabs on top!

"Mmmm. . ." said Horatio, licking
his lips. He didn't know where to start.

"Who's hungry, then?" Aunt Marigold
asked, and lots of fluffy paws shot up.

"*Me!*" cried everyone, even little Daisy,
who seemed much happier now they
were back in the cosy, familiar cottage.

They all sat around the table but

before they tucked in, the friends gave Aunt Marigold some thank-you presents they'd brought.

Riley's was some jars of home-made jam and Horatio had brought a big bottle of lemonade he'd made with his dad last week. He also gave Daisy one of his prize-winning conkers.

Starla had a dried flower garland to hang on the front door. It was made of wild roses and dainty purple violets. "All of the flowers came from my garden!" she beamed.

Afternoon tea began and it tasted as yummy as it looked. Everyone had a

little bit of everything. Then Horatio had
a little bit more!

"Mmmm. . ." said Uncle Norton, when
the cakes had all gone. He patted his
tummy and smiled. "So, who would like
a little play on the beach?"

"Me!" squeaked Riley.

"Yes, please," Starla nodded.

"Hooray!" Horatio cheered.

"What about you, Daisy?" asked her mum.

"I-I. . ." stuttered Daisy, her whiskers twitching. She looked quite unsure again.

"Go on," coaxed her dad. "It'll be fun!"

"Well . . . all right, then," Daisy murmured.

Starla clapped her paws. "Yippee!"

Aunt Marigold and Grandpa were staying in for a chat, but the others went off with Uncle Norton. Riley noticed a parcel tucked under his arm, and as soon as they got to the sand, Uncle Norton held it out.

"Here," he said. "A little something for you."

"Oh, I *love* little somethings!" beamed Horatio.

"Can we open it now, Uncle Norton?" asked Riley.

"Of course!"

The present had been wrapped in white sail fabric and tied with stripey red and white string. On the top sat some sea-holly to make it look extra pretty.

"Well," chuckled Uncle Norton, "what are you waiting for?"

Riley took the parcel and popped it

on the sand. Then everyone unwrapped
it together.

"Wow, Uncle Norton!" Riley gasped.
"Thanks!"

Their present was a lovely green
dragon kite with a big friendly smile.

"Let's call it Dylan!" Starla cried. "Like our dragon steam train!"

"But it's too windy to fly a kite!" gasped Daisy.

"No it's not," said Riley.

"It will be OK," Uncle Norton nodded.

So everyone took it in turns to fly Dylan. All except Daisy, who watched. Every two minutes she licked her paw and held it up to check the wind.

"Too windy," she muttered, shaking her head. "Too windy!"

Uncle Norton kept trying to get Daisy to join in but she flatly refused. Horatio, though, was having a *wonderful* time. . .

"Yippee! Look at me!" he cried as he bounded off along the sand, pulling the kite behind him.

"Hey, Horatio," Riley giggled. "Not so fast!"

Next Starla had a go and she made Dylan dive and twirl. Finally it was Riley's turn. He gripped the kite's string and let it out slowly so that Dylan soared high into the air.

"Look, Daisy," said Horatio. "There's nothing to worry about, see?"

But no sooner had he said those words than a big gust of wind blew in off the sea. Both Dylan *and* Riley were swept into the sky.

"Arggh!" yelled Riley. "Uncle Norton!
Get me down!"

With a shriek, Riley's uncle sprang
through the air, grabbing hold of Riley's
foot and pulling him back down to
the sand.

"I'm fine!" said Riley quickly, as Horatio, Starla and Daisy dashed over.

"See!" said Daisy. "It's too windy for kites! I told you."

She suggested they all do something a bit safer, so they set about digging a long, wiggly tunnel and filled it with water from the sea. Daisy lent them her bucket but didn't want to pour in case she got muddy or wet.

"Look," cried Horatio, "we're making a swamp!"

"Let's be Hopping Frogs!" said Riley.

"*Plop*," giggled Starla, jumping in.

When the big yellow sun had turned

to deepest orange, it was time to go in for supper. In the cottage the lanterns had all been lit and a yummy nut roast was being brought to the table. "Holidays really are the best thing *ever*!" grinned Horatio.

After supper it was time for bed. From his bunk Riley noticed the pattern of little crabs all over the pale blue curtains. He might even catch a *real* crab tomorrow, fingers crossed!

Chapter 3

The next morning Riley woke to the song of seagulls and the gentle splash of the sea. It was time for lots more playing on the beach!

He hurried down his ladder and tickled Horatio awake with a feather from his pillow. "Last one downstairs is a pongy old kipper!" laughed Riley.

The boys raced down to have their breakfast. Starla and Daisy were already in the kitchen, along with Grandpa Lightfoot.

He was reading his newspaper in a chair by the open window.

"Hello!" called the boys. Then Riley looked around. "Where's Uncle Norton?"

"Daddy's already gone to work," said Daisy.

Riley told his friends that his uncle was a potter and made lovely things out of clay.

"Daddy made that jug," Daisy said, pointing to the big white jug filled with catmint. "And all our cups and bowls and plates as well!"

Aunt Marigold had cooked a big stack of pancakes which they dribbled with thick

golden syrup. Then they each had a drink
of milk from Uncle Norton's striped mugs.

After breakfast they got washed and
put on their beach clothes. Then Riley

raced to the door. "Come on!" he cried. "Let's go and play on the beach!"

Starla and Horatio hurried over but Daisy wasn't too sure. What if Riley got blown away again?

"We could stay in and play with my seals?" said Daisy.

"Nah!" cried Horatio. "Let's go out!"

Grandpa tried to persuade Daisy to go. "We could collect shells," he said to her.

"Oooh yes!" said Starla, picking up her rucksack. "I promised Mimi-Rose I'd take her some nice ones home."

Quick as a flash, Aunt Marigold appeared holding two bright buckets.

"You could collect them in these, Daisy,"
she smiled.

Daisy thought for a moment. "Well,
maybe. . ." she said. She did like shells
very much.

"Hurrah!" cried Horatio, opening the
door. "Let's go!"

Grandpa and Daisy took the buckets.
"Oh wait!" said Grandpa. "We need
these too!"

He handed out new fishing nets
he'd made back home in Willow Valley.
Riley had a red one, Horatio's was green,
Starla's was lilac and Daisy's was blue
because blue was her favourite colour.

Aunt Marigold picked up the picnic basket she had filled with nice things for lunch, and then Horatio led them out through the door.

Outside a warm breeze danced on the air and the sand was buttercup yellow. Although it was early, the beach was quite busy. Some squirrels and moles were splashing in the sea, while bunnies filled their buckets with seaweed. And lots of little badgers were digging tunnels.

"Let's go rock pooling!" Riley cried.

"Good idea!" smiled Aunt Marigold.

"But there might be *crabs*," Daisy gasped.

"Who cares!" cried Horatio. "Crabs are OK!"

"There might be good seashells too. . ." said Starla.

"Come on, Daisy, it'll be fine!" Grandpa smiled.

Armed with their nets, they found some rock pools which twinkled in the bright sun. Riley wondered what they'd fish out. It felt just like a game of lucky dip!

They took it in turns to pop their nets in the water. Horatio went first and to his delight, he fished out a big hermit crab. It had a hard brown shell and big pinchy claws.

"I think he looks a bit cross," said Riley.

"He doesn't," grinned Horatio. "He's smiling, look!"

He picked up the crab and examined him more closely. "Hello, Mr Crab. I'm Horatio!" he said.

"Don't hold him so close to your face," Starla warned, but Horatio paid no attention.

"He's OK," Horatio beamed. "He likes me!"

With that, the crab shot out a claw and pinched Horatio hard on the nose.

"Ow!" yelled Horatio, as the crab dangled down. *"Get off!"*

Grandpa Lightfoot prised open the

crab's big claw, then popped him down on the sand. Horatio's poor nose was throbbing like mad. "Mean old, pinchy old, horrible *beastie*!" he frowned.

It was Starla's turn to go fishing now. She placed her net into the rock pool and scooped out some stones and a beautiful starfish. "Oooh!" she smiled, showing it off. "It's lovely!"

Riley went next and found three spider crabs hiding in a big clump of seaweed. They were cream coloured and had long spindly legs, like a spider.

Finally, it was Daisy's turn. She fished out a whelk and some pearly seashells.

"Oh, so pretty!" said her mum, as they sparkled like jewels.

Grandpa Lightfoot then gathered everyone together. He explained that they had to put the creatures back *exactly* where they had found them. "You see, that rock pool is their home," he said, "until the tide comes back in."

"Well, I'm not touching that crab again!" scowled Horatio.

So Riley's grandpa popped the crab back for him and soon all the creatures were back in their watery home.

To cheer Horatio up, Grandpa took them to the sea to have a little paddle

in the water. Starla wore her flowery
rubber ring and the boys both wore
their armbands. Daisy wore her rubber
ring too, but just wanted to watch.

Riley and his friends tiptoed into the
water. "It's *cold*!" giggled Starla.

"F-freezing!" shivered the boys.

After a while they got used to it
and raced in and out squealing as tiny
waves chased them up the sand.

Eventually Daisy felt brave enough
to dip her toes in the water. "Oooh,
it's tickly!" she said with a giggle. She
couldn't remember the last time she'd
been in the sea.

Everyone paddled over to her. At
last, thought Riley, she was having
some fun! It didn't last very long,
though. . .

"Come and jump over the waves!"
said Starla.

"Oh, no!" gasped Daisy. "I might fall in!" And she scooted back out of the water and over to Grandpa.

"Why won't she *try* things?" Horatio said, whooshing some water at Riley.

"Oi!" laughed Riley, splashing him back.

"Hee hee!" giggled Starla, and *she* joined in too. "Water fight!"

While the three friends splashed about in the water, they rather forgot about Daisy. They were far too busy having a wonderful time!

After their paddle, everyone had lunch. Then it was playtime again. "Let's dig holes," Starla suggested. She loved digging holes and was good at it too, having such great big paws.

"OK," said Horatio.

"Let's dig for treasure!" cried Riley.

They charged down the sand and started to dig, forgetting about Daisy again. So Grandpa took her for a stroll with him while Aunt Marigold tidied away the picnic.

Before long the boys had dug so deep they'd reached soggy sand. "Faster, Horatio!" Riley cried. But nobody could dig as fast as Starla.

"Wheee!" she cried, as sand flew up around her. And soon she'd disappeared down the hole!

Then suddenly the digging stopped and Starla's head popped out. "Hey," she said, "I think I've found some treasure!"

The boys hurried over. "What is it?" asked Riley.

"Ooh!" cried Horatio, pointing a paw. "I can see it!"

The corner of what looked like an old silver brooch was poking out of the sand. Starla pulled it out but something much bigger came with it.

"Ha! Funny treasure!" Horatio snorted, as Starla waved a sandy old boot. It was brown and wrinkly with a dull silver buckle on the side.

Starla tossed the boot to Horatio. He tipped out the sand, pulled it on, then started hopping about.

"Grrr! I'm a one-legged pirate!" he chuckled. "Oooh arggh!"

Later, when Daisy and Grandpa got back, the others were all playing leapfrog. Daisy held up a big bucket of shells. "We'll look at them after our game!" Riley called over.

But after the game the friends played catch, then hide-and-seek, then rounders. No one asked Daisy if *she* wanted to play because they *knew* that she wouldn't. So Riley, Horatio and Starla played together until it was time to go in. . .

At supper Uncle Norton wanted to hear all about their day.

"We fished, and splashed, and even found treasure!" grinned Riley.

"Did *you* have fun?" Uncle Norton asked Daisy.

Daisy gave a little shrug. "I just found some shells. . ." she answered quietly.

As everyone pattered up to bed, Grandpa called Riley over. "I know Daisy worries about . . . lots," he said, "but you mustn't leave her out."

"I didn't!" frowned Riley. But then he thought. "Well, I didn't *mean* to. . ." And he promised Grandpa he would do his best not to leave Daisy out tomorrow.

"Good lad," Grandpa smiled. "Now off to bed. We've got *caves* to explore in the morning!"

Riley nodded excitedly. "Hooray!"

Chapter 4

Breakfast the next morning was boiled eggs and toasty soldiers. Grandpa and the girls were already at the table when Riley and Horatio pattered in. The boys sat down and Aunt Marigold brought over their eggs.

"I'm staying home today," Daisy said, looking very glum indeed.

"Oh," said Grandpa. "That's a pity – we're going to the caves!"

Daisy quickly shook her head. "Much too spooky."

Horatio tutted and Starla sighed.
Daisy wouldn't try *anything*. If she
carried on like this, she was going to
ruin their holiday!

"You could borrow my torch, Daisy?"
Riley said, remembering his promise to
Grandpa. "It'll make the caves nice and
bright, and then you won't be scared."

"Oh!" said Aunt Marigold. "Isn't that
kind?" She patted Riley's head and
beamed.

"Would you like that, Daisy?" Grandpa
asked, giving Riley a quick thank-you
wink.

"Um. . ." said Daisy.

"Go on!" smiled her mum. "Grandpa will look after you and I'll bring you a picnic at lunchtime."

"Er. . ." said Daisy, her whiskers quivering. She thought for a moment then uttered a nervous "OK."

So Riley found his torch and gave it to her. Then Daisy kissed her mum goodbye and went outside with the others. The sand was warm and little seagulls circled overhead.

Riley found everyone a stick to lean on while they walked to the caves. "*All* explorers have knobbly sticks!" he nodded.

Daisy was quiet all the way to the caves. When they got there, her bottom lip was trembling and she looked like she might cry.

"I don't want to!" she squeaked suddenly. "I want to go home!" She shook her little head. "Caves scare me!"

"Perhaps we should do something else?" said Grandpa, as Daisy gave a teary sniff.

The friends all groaned. She was being a worry-wart *again*. . .

"Please, Daisy," begged Riley. "It'll be great!"

But Daisy shook her head.

"Can *we* still go in, Grandpa?" asked Riley. "Horatio, Starla and me." He crossed his fingers tightly. "*Please!*"

There were three caves, two small ones and one much bigger. Grandpa took a quick look inside each of them as the others waited with Daisy.

"All right," said Grandpa, finally. "You can play in the caves for a bit. But in the big one there's a wobbly pile of rocks, so no climbing up it, OK?"

"OK," said Riley, Starla and Horatio. "We won't!"

Grandpa stayed outside with Daisy as the others raced into the biggest cave. "Wow!" cried Riley when they got inside. *"Cool."*

The cave was deep and echoey and water dripped and plopped. It wasn't as dark as Riley had imagined and he wasn't scared in the slightest. Neither were Starla and Horatio – they *loved* it!

They pretended they were knights
again and went searching for the sea
monster. As they searched, Horatio
spotted a big mound of seaweed. Then
Starla suddenly had a brilliant idea. . .

"Hey, let's play seaweed-tag!" she cried. And she quickly explained the rules. "You two must be pirates, and jump from rock to rock. And I'll try and splat you with seaweed!"

"Yippee!" cheered the boys. Seaweed-tag sounded *amazing*.

The game began and it was such fun. Riley and Horatio leapt about from rock to rock, and Starla tried to splat them with seaweed.

"Eeek!" squeaked Riley, when a bit hit his chin. "Who likes my slimy green beard?"

"Hey!" laughed Horatio. "I've got

one too! Hee hee!"

The game went on until Horatio decided to make a *cannonball* out of seaweed. He hurled it through the air. "Wheee!" he bellowed. "Watch out!"

Riley and Starla squealed excitedly, but neither were watching where the slimy cannonball was heading, *until. . .*

SPLAT!

The big ball of seaweed had landed right on Starla, covering her all over in drippy green goo.

"Ewww!" she screamed. Then she

looked at herself and a grin spread
across her face.

"*I'm a grumpy sea monster!*" she roared
in a gruff, grumbly voice. And she
squelched forward to get the boys. . .

"*Raaaghhh!*"

When everyone was quite puffed out, they headed back outside. The friends had never been messier, or happier!

Grandpa and Daisy were drawing pictures in the sand with their explorers' sticks.

"That was *so* much fun!" snorted Riley, showing Grandpa his slimy green paws.

"Goodness!" chuckled Grandpa. "Look at the state of you!"

He took them to the sea and they washed off the seaweed. Then Riley said that Daisy should choose the next game because she'd waited patiently while they'd played in the cave.

"I'd like us all to build a sandcastle!" said Daisy.

Everyone liked the sound of that, so they found a good spot and got started. It was nice to do something a bit calmer now, and Daisy was very good at building castles.

They worked together and took great care and, bit by bit, the castle was built. They made turrets, then drew doors and windows using thin sticks or the pointy ends of feathers.

Starla said she'd brought some flags from home. She found them in her rucksack and they popped them on the turrets, where they fluttered in the gentle breeze.

Finally everyone dug a deep moat, which went right around the castle. "This place is fit for a king!" Horatio smiled.

Riley suggested to Daisy that they put some shells on it too, and Daisy really liked this idea. They were about to go off and find some when Aunt Marigold appeared with a picnic basket.

"We'll find the shells straight after lunch!" Riley promised Daisy.

Aunt Marigold laid down a picnic rug and unpacked her basket of goodies. There were boat-shaped banana sandwiches and pasties that looked like shells. There were cupcakes too, the tops of which had been iced with little mermaids. Even the cubes of cheese looked like mini sandcastles!

After lunch Aunt Marigold had to nip home to make something special for later.

"OK," said Riley, "let's get started on those shells!"

"I think it'll look jolly smart," said Grandpa. "And while you're all busy doing that, I'm just going to pop home too to find a good, strong basket."

He said he needed it to collect some driftwood. Back home in Willow Valley he ran the toyshop and he wanted to take some wood home to make new toys.

"Now, while I'm gone," Grandpa said, "you mustn't go into the sea. A grown-up should always watch you in the water."

"OK," everyone nodded.

Grandpa left and they began to look for shells. They wanted to fill their buckets right up!

"I'm going to find some pebbles too," said Horatio.

Swinging his bucket, he headed up the beach, but he hadn't gone far when he stopped. A little way out at sea was a rock. A big grey rock. Earlier, when they'd been washing off their seaweed, this rock had been quite bare. Now, though, something was sitting on it.

"What's on that rock?" Horatio said, squinting his eyes to see.

"Oh my!" gasped Starla. "I think it might be . . . a *mermaid*!"

Chapter 5

"A mermaid?" said Horatio excitedly. But it was too far away to see. "Let's go and get a closer look!" he cried.

They left their sandcastle and ran down the sand. "But we mustn't go in the water," said Daisy.

"We won't!"

Daisy liked the sound of mermaids on her beach. She would come more often if she had a *friend* to play with, and a magical friend could protect her from all sorts of danger. . .

As they got nearer the water's edge, the thing on the rock became clearer. It wasn't a mermaid after all.

"Look," said Riley. "It's a seal!"

"A seal!" squealed Daisy. "Oooh – it *is*! It's a *mummy* seal, look! I love seals even more than mermaids! I never knew they lived on *my* beach, though."

The mummy seal's coat was silvery grey and shimmered like the moon. Her deep dark eyes were like two shiny drops of ink.

"But she looks a bit worried," Daisy said. The mummy seal's whiskers were all of a quiver as she gazed out to sea.

"*Hello!*" called Riley from the water's
edge.

"Starla thought you were a mermaid!"
cried Horatio.

"I think she's looking for something,"
Starla said.

The mummy seal glanced across at them. Then her eyes shot again to the water.

"Have you lost something?" Daisy called to her.

"Yes!" cried the mummy seal. "Have you seen him?"

"Seen who?" asked Riley.

"Alfie," the mummy seal replied.

She explained how Alfie, her baby boy, had been swimming beside her in the water. "Then I stopped to show him a sweet little gull calling to us from the sky, but when I looked down again," she said, "Alfie was gone."

Alfie's mummy swam to them through

big, tumbling waves. The tide was coming in fast now. "Maybe he's been washed ashore?" she said.

"What does he look like?" Daisy asked. "Is he soft and white like my teddy seal, Twinkle?"

"As soft as a snowflake," Alfie's mummy answered. "And his eyes are deep and dark." She peered around the busy beach, but Alfie was nowhere to be seen.

"We could help you look?" offered Starla.

"We'll find him!" cried the boys. But Daisy had suddenly gone very quiet.

"What's wrong, Daisy?" Riley asked.

"I just . . . I'd like to help too,"
replied Daisy. "But big adventures like
this make me scared."

"Come on, we'll look after you!" said
Riley.

Daisy's whiskers twitched as she
thought very hard. . .

"OK," she said finally. "I'll look for
Alfie too!"

They split up and checked different
parts of the beach. Riley and Daisy
searched the sand dunes, while Starla
and Horatio asked around in case anyone
had spotted a baby seal. But it was no
good. No one had seen little Alfie.

Then Alfie's mummy spied an old
rowing boat lying upside down on the
sand. She peeped under it just in case
Alfie was playing hide-and-seek. But no,
there were just a few scuttling crabs and
some seaweed.

Now the caves were the only place left to search. Alfie's mummy said she should check the sea again too.

As she hurried back into the water, Riley led everyone to the caves. "Come on!" he called. He felt like a real explorer!

They decided to check the smallest cave first. They hurried over, but just before they went in, Daisy said someone should stay outside to keep a lookout for Grandpa. "If he comes back and no one's here, he'll be worried!" she said.

Everyone agreed, so Daisy stayed outside while the others searched the first cave.

"No sign of Alfie," said Riley, as they trooped back outside.

They went into the second cave, and again Daisy waited outside. They searched it carefully, but Alfie wasn't in there either.

That just left the biggest cave but now the tide was coming in fast. This cave was the one they'd played in earlier, so they knew it very well. They raced inside while Daisy waited for Grandpa.

This cave was the gloomiest of them all and it had lots of rocks and shady corners. "We must still search every bit!" Riley told his friends.

They split up and searched around every rock. Then they checked all the gloomy corners.

Finally they all met up. "It's no good," said Starla, shaking her head. "He's not here."

Suddenly they heard Daisy call from outside, but they couldn't make out what she was saying.

"She sounds worried," said Starla. "I wonder what's wrong."

"Probably nothing," Horatio frowned. "Daisy *always* sounds worried."

Riley shrugged. "Come on, we'd better go. . ."

The friends turned to leave, but as they did, a flash of white caught Starla's eye. "Look!" she gasped, pointing up. *"It's Alfie!"*

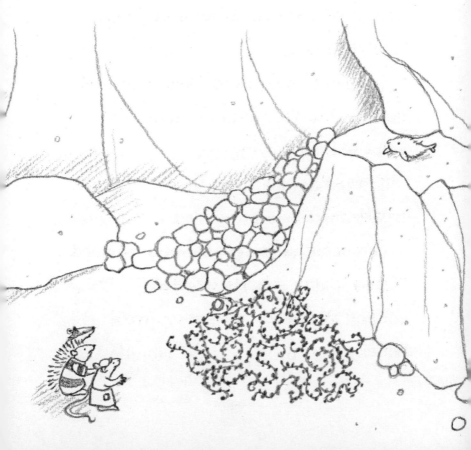

The baby seal lay trembling on a craggy ledge halfway up the cave wall. "How did he get up there?" asked Horatio.

"Up those rocks, I bet," said Starla, pointing to the pile of wobbly rocks.

"Alfie. . ." Riley called gently, "can you climb back down?" But Alfie's deep dark eyes were wide with fear.

"I think he must be scared of heights," whispered Starla.

With that, they heard Daisy call again. She sounded really frightened.

"The sea!" came Daisy's voice. "It's coming! *Quick*!"

"I bet it's not *that* close," Horatio

tutted. Daisy was probably just fussing again.

"Come on, Alfie!" Riley called. But Alfie was too frightened to move. Riley knew he would have to help him down.

He raced to the wobbly pile of rocks and began to scramble up them.

"Riley! What are you *doing*?" gasped Starla. "Your grandpa said not to go near those rocks when we came this morning."

"But someone needs to get Alfie down!" said Riley.

Carefully he clambered up the rocks as Starla and Horatio watched.

"Steady!" called Starla.

"*I'm OK!*" puffed Riley.

Finally he reached the craggy ledge where the baby seal sat quivering.

"Here, Alfie," said Riley. "Hold my paw."

Alfie blinked. Then, ever so slowly, he reached out a little flipper. Riley was just about to take it when a sudden rumbling filled the cave. It sounded like a great angry giant had woken.

Then in rushed the sea. . .

WHOOSH!

Starla and Horatio climbed on to a big rock as the water gushed in around them.

"Riley!" Starla called, looking down at the water. "We need to get out of this cave!"

"OK!" Riley nodded. He turned back to Alfie. "Come on, Alfie – we can do it!"

Chapter 6

As Alfie trembled on the ledge, another wave of water swept into the cave. But this time something *else* came with it. . .

"Mummy! Mummy!" Alfie cried. "My mummy!"

Alfie's mummy looked up at him as she bobbed about in the water. "Alfie," she called, "take the mouse's paw and come to Mummy!"

Alfie took hold of Riley's paw and they began their journey down the rocks. "Alfie," said Riley firmly, "don't look down."

Alfie did as he was told as the water got deeper and deeper. "Good boy, Alfie!" his mummy called. "That's it!"

Finally, Riley and Alfie reached the rock where Starla and Horatio stood out of the water.

"Now then, Alfie," said his mummy, "jump!"

She counted to three and Alfie jumped. *"Wheee!"* he giggled as he landed in the water.

SPLOSH!

Alfie's mummy swam close to him and held on to his flipper but she noticed the water looked very deep now.

"Can you all swim?" she asked the friends.

"I can!" said Horatio. "But only with my armbands."

"Me too," Riley nodded.

"And I need my rubber ring," Starla sighed.

Suddenly they heard an echoing cry and *another* wave swept into the cave, along with an old rowing boat! It was captained by a little mouse.

Riley could hardly believe his eyes. *"Look,"* he gasped. *"It's Daisy!"*

Daisy rowed over with all her might and the friends clambered into the boat. Daisy looked shocked at her own reckless daring. She didn't know *where*

she had found the courage to lead an exciting rescue. She must have been much braver than she'd thought!

"Wow!" gasped Starla.

"Thanks, Daisy," said Riley, as he helped her turn the boat around.

"Brave Pirate Daisy to the rescue!" Horatio cheered.

Slowly but surely the little boat bobbed its way out of the cave. Riley took one of the oars whilst Daisy had the other. Behind them was Alfie on his mummy's back as she helped to nudge the boat along with her nose.

When they got outside they quickly

rowed to shallow water. They climbed out of the boat and were dragging it ashore when they heard a frightened cry. . .

"*Children!*"

It was Aunt Marigold. She came racing up with Grandpa.

"Goodness!" she panted. "What's been going on?"

"This is Alfie!" said Daisy quickly. "And this is Alfie's mummy."

Then she and Horatio told how Alfie had got lost and they had helped to find him. (Except Horatio added bits about pirates and sharks, which no one – except *him* – could remember!)

"But you shouldn't have gone off by *yourselves*," said Grandpa. "You should have come to find us! Going into caves when an adult's not there is very dangerous, you know."

Grandpa shook his head. "I'm very

disappointed in you all."

"It's really my fault," said Alfie's mum. "I was so worried about my baby! But I shouldn't have let them help at all. I'm so sorry."

Aunt Marigold looked at her. "You must have been very frightened."

"I was – so, *so* frightened," said Alfie's mum.

Riley now noticed Grandpa, whose whiskers were all of a quiver. *He* looked very frightened too. "We're sorry, Grandpa," Riley said.

"We really didn't mean to scare you," said Starla.

Meanwhile, Alfie had sidled up to Daisy. He had never met anyone so fearless before. "Brave Daisy!" he beamed. And he gave her a hug.

"Hey, Daisy," said Riley, "I think you've just made a new friend!"

Aunt Marigold knelt down on the sand and took Daisy's paws in her own. "You did a very brave thing," she said. "But you know you should never go into the water by yourself *ever* again."

"I know," said Daisy, nodding her head. "But I'd like to go into the sea with *you*. The water was fun when it tickled my toes before. . ."

Daisy then said goodbye to Alfie, but promised to come and see him every day. And Alfie's mum promised that they would always be waiting. . .

It was time to go home, and as they headed to the cottage, a dreamy smell wafted down to meet them.

"I baked you a treat," Aunt Marigold said. "Though I'm not really sure you deserve it now."

"But we're really sorry!" Riley said as they walked up the garden path.

"We've learned our lesson," Starla nodded.

"And we're *ever* so hungry," gasped Horatio.

Slowly, Aunt Marigold nodded. "All right then."

Grandpa opened the door and they

pattered in, where an enormous ginger cake was waiting.

"Mmmm. . ." beamed Horatio, licking his lips. "My *favourite!*"

They washed their paws and sat at the table.

"So, what shall we do tomorrow?" asked Riley, his cheeks bulging with cake. There were still days and days of holiday left!

"I know – let's visit the *lighthouse*," said Daisy.

"That sounds good," smiled Starla.

"But . . . isn't it meant to be haunted?" asked Riley. There were stories that the big old lighthouse had ghosts.

"That's just what people say," shrugged Daisy. "I don't think it's haunted really."

"Anyway, *we're* not scared of ghosts!" grinned Horatio.

After tea, they all chatted about the exciting seaside rescue. And tomorrow sounded *just* as exciting. All thanks to brave little Daisy!

Look out for more

stories — out now!

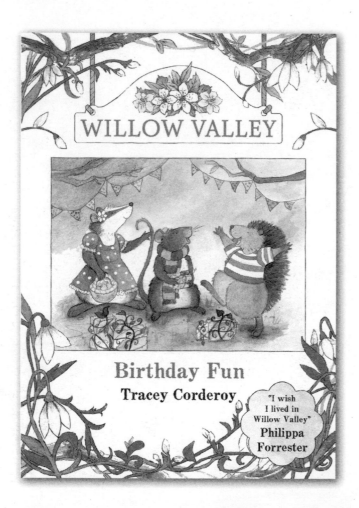

WILLOW VALLEY

Birthday Fun

Tracey Corderoy

"I wish
I lived in
Willow Valley"
**Philippa
Forrester**

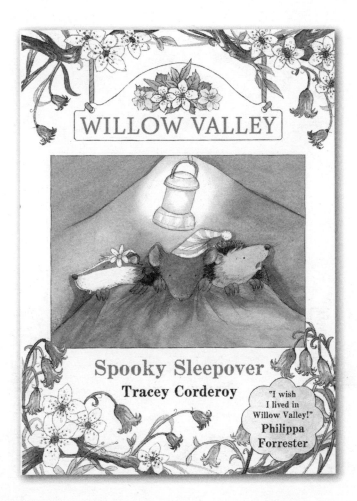

WILLOW VALLEY

Spooky Sleepover

Tracey Corderoy

"I wish
I lived in
Willow Valley!"
**Philippa
Forrester**

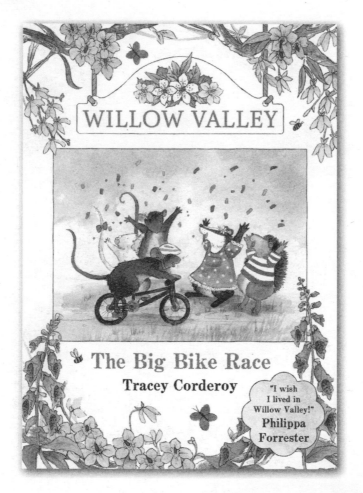

WILLOW VALLEY

The Big Bike Race

Tracey Corderoy

"I wish
I lived in
Willow Valley!"
**Philippa
Forrester**

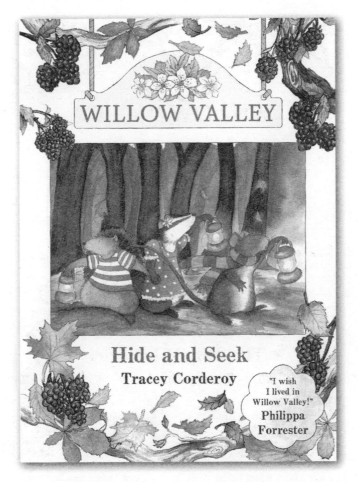

Hide and Seek
Tracey Corderoy

"I wish
I lived in
Willow Valley!"
**Philippa
Forrester**

WILLOW VALLEY

One Snowy Day

Tracey Corderoy

"I wish
I lived in
Willow Valley!"
**Philippa
Forrester**

Coming Soon

WILLOW VALLEY

Toffee Apple Night
Tracey Corderoy

"I wish
I lived in
Willow Valley!"
**Philippa
Forrester**